Sheep Go to Sleep

Nancy Shaw

Sheep Go to Sleep

Illustrated by Margot Apple

Houghton Mifflin Harcourt
Boston   New York

For Margaret Raymo, and in memory of Matilda Welter,
with thanks for suggesting this sheep adventure. — N.S.

For my grandmother friends and their boys:
Dominic Xavier Kofler & Anne Kofler
Samuel Anthony Visser & Sally Boutiette — M.A.

Text copyright © 2015 by Nancy Shaw
Illustrations copyright © 2015 by Margot Apple

www.hmhco.com

The text of this book is set in Garamond.
The illustrations are colored pencil.

Library of Congress Cataloging-in-Publication Data
Shaw, Nancy (Nancy E.)
Sheep go to sleep / by Nancy Shaw ; illustrated by Margot Apple.
pages cm
Summary: At the end of the day, tired sheep return to their shed but none can
sleep until the collie arrives, giving a hug, a drink of water, and more until all
have begun to snore.
ISBN 978-0-544-30989-0
[1. Stories in rhyme. 2. Bedtime—Fiction. 3. Sheep—Fiction. 4. Collies—
Fiction. 5. Dogs—Fiction.] I. Apple, Margot, illustrator. II. Title.
PZ8.3.S5334Sgv 2015
[E]—dc23
2014009947

Manufactured in China
SCP 10 9 8 7 6 5 4 3 2 1
4500517642

Winking fireflies light the way,
as sheep stroll home to hit the hay.

Five sheep settle in their shed,
using straw to make the bed.

Screeches! Rustling! Noisy crickets!
Sheep hear hoots from nearby thickets.

Nighttime noises scare the sheep.
Really, who could go to sleep?

Sheep bleat. Sheep sigh.

A trusty collie wanders by.

What would make the sheep feel snug?

The collie gives a sheep a hug.

The tired sheep begins to snore.

One asleep! How many more?

One sheep asks to have a drink.

The collie gets it from the sink.

Another sheep begins to snore.

Two asleep! How many more?

A lullaby should calm the flock.
Sheep tap rhythm, hum, and rock.

Another sheep begins to snore.
Three asleep! How many more?

One sheep wants a teddy bear.
The collie brings his own to share.

Another sheep begins to snore.
Four asleep! How many more?

The last one wants a cozy quilt
to snuggle in the bed she built.

The collie gives a weary grin.
He fetches one and tucks her in.

All the sheep have closed their eyes.

They'll drowse and dream until sunrise.

But where is the dog who looks after the sheep?

He's under the haystack, fast asleep.